Caleb's
Lamb

Caleb's Lamb

Helen Santos

REFORMATION HERITAGE BOOKS
Grand Rapids, Michigan

Copyright © Helen Santos

Published by
Reformation Heritage Books
2965 Leonard St., NE
Grand Rapids, MI 49525
616-977-0599 / Fax 616-285-3246
e-mail: orders@heritagebooks.org
website: www.heritagebooks.org

10 digit ISBN # 1-892777-70-3
13 digit ISBN # 978-1-892-777-70-6

Originally published by
Scripture Union, 1984

RHB edition
First Printing 2005
Second Printing 2007

Cover photo of boy: Nik Wheeler

*For additional Reformed literature, both new and used,
request a free book list from the above address.*

Preface

Caleb's Lamb was given to us by a friend to read to our children. Already from the first chapter, our family was fascinated by the way in which the author, Helen Santos, drew us into the story. Upon further reading, the real meaning and depth of what this book was about amazed us even more. It was then that we realized this book needed to be shared with others.

The publisher was contacted in order to purchase some copies, only to find it was out of print and that the copyright had been reverted back to the author. Therefore, the only way of getting more copies would be through her. After much searching, in God's marvelous providence, the author was located in Bath, England. We spoke with her and explained our desire to publish this fascinating book as a fundraiser for our newly begun Christian school. We were overjoyed to have her tell us that she too would like to see Christian education furthered and would give us the sole rights to publish this edition of *Caleb's Lamb*.

Helen Santos said the following regarding the birth of this book: "I originally wrote this story in episodes for a summer children's club here in Bath and later turned it into a book. The children all enjoyed it then— a long time ago—and I very much hope it will benefit the children who will be reading it today. For me, it's a privilege to use my writing ability in the Lord's service and I pray that this story might help and encourage children to know and love Jesus and the Bible."

Above all, we wish to acknowledge the Lord for directing this book to us. We pray that this little book may not only raise money for our school, but may be blessed to the hearts of all who read this story, both young and old alike. We also heartily thank Helen Santos for allowing us to published this book without remuneration, and Reformation Heritage Books for publishing it. Lastly, a special thanks is extended to all those who have put their time and talents into preparing this book for print.

— Rev. and Mrs. Mark Kelderman
Members of the Oxford
Reformed Christian School

~ 1 ~

A long, long time ago, in the land of Goshen in Egypt, a young lad was lying fast asleep at the foot of a thorn tree. To keep wild animals away, he had pulled a few loose branches about himself. To keep warm, he had curled himself up as small as he could under his father's tatty cloak.

The sun had been up for more than an hour, warming the earth, but the boy had spent half the night awake, filled with fear, so now his sleep was still deep. The bright light of full dawn had not disturbed it.

A raven was perched on a high branch of the same thorn tree, jerking his head from one side to another as each eye in turn kept watch on the boy below. He sidled up and down the branch, trying to get a better view, intensely curious. In the end he let out a loud, harsh cry, which broke into the boy's sleep.

The cloak was thrown back and a tousled dark head appeared, sleepy eyes unwillingly opening, then widening with fear as the boy remembered where he was and that he was alone.

He sat up, pressing his back against the tree, and pulled the cloak around him again, shivering. Although the sun was up it wasn't a hot sun. The time was early spring and there was still a bite in the air.

Caleb was wearing a sheepskin jacket over his tunic, as well as the cloak which belonged to his father, but the ground was as cold as it was hard.

His brown eyes glanced up at the raven in the tree. It was surely a bad omen that such a bird should be sitting there, watching him. Its long, black beak reminded him that this was a beak for tearing and stabbing. The curved, black talons, clinging now to the branch, could cling just as fiercely to an injured creature. The sharp, piercing eyes already seemed to gloat.

Caleb jumped up, suddenly angry. He waved his arms and shouted at the raven, "Go away. Go away. Don't stare at me like that." But the raven stared with even greater curiosity, unafraid.

It was Caleb's guilt that made him so angry at the sight of the raven. Just as soon as he woke up, memories of the previous day came rushing back . . . his father's anger, his own, the lost ewe. . . .

Oh, how he hated the sheep. Stupid animals. Didn't they know by now that the only safe place was in the flock, under the shepherd's care? Didn't they know by now that at night-time they should hurry to the fold?

Obviously they didn't, because if they did they wouldn't wander off and get lost.

Caleb's father, Asher, had said, "That ewe will be lambing soon. Any day now. Keep an eye on her. She'll be wandering off to find a secret place to give birth. You must watch her carefully and bring her back if she strays."

And Caleb had watched. He really had. He'd watched her for hours, until the sun made his eyes ache and the strain of keeping his gaze fixed on her brown, woolly rump and long, fat tail made him dizzy and tired.

He'd only stopped watching her for a little while. She was with several of her sisters, nibbling at the new spring grass, perfectly content. And a lizard had come jerking out from under the rocks—a tiny thing with golden eyes, so tempting to his idle fingers, so promising to his weary heart....

It was as still as the rocks themselves, easy to catch. Caleb cupped his hands—and in a flash it was gone, just as soon as his shadow moved. Caleb pulled up rocks, drawn on by the twitch of a tail.... There it was again, head in the air, frozen and beautiful.

It was only a moment, but when Caleb remembered the ewe and looked to the place where he had last seen her, the rest were there, still nibbling, but the brown one with bulging sides had gone.

Caleb tried not to panic. He knew he must find her quickly, but he didn't dare start running about in case his father noticed. She couldn't have gone very far. Perhaps she'd moved into a bunch under his father's eyes. The whole flock was straggled out, over a wide stretch of grazing, some already with lambs tagging along beside.

But how could he tell which was the one he was looking for? There were a number of brown sheep in the flock, as well as grey, white, and spotted ones. His father said each one was different, but they all looked alike to him.

How angry Caleb felt with the brown ewe. How angry he felt with his father. How could he watch them every single minute, when his head ached and his eyes watered? He knew he should have gone to tell his father, there and then, but he didn't. He was too ashamed and angry.

Only that morning Asher had given him a lecture on the importance of watching the lambing ewes extra carefully. It wasn't a long lecture. Shepherds aren't used to talking much, though they often sing to their sheep. But just because his father didn't say much, the words he used when he did speak were important and had to be listened to.

Three times he had told Caleb to watch that particular ewe, so how could Caleb go to his father now and tell him that she was lost?

Caleb had decided to wait a while, certain she would come back before nightfall, bringing a lamb with her. Then his father need never know what had happened. But the day had worn on and she hadn't returned, and as the time went by it became harder and harder to tell. Asher might have been angry at the beginning. He would be even angrier now.

Caleb dutifully watched the remaining sheep for the rest of the day, expecting a miracle to happen at any moment—the brown sheep trotting back with a lamb at foot.

He had thought about praying to his father's God about it. Every morning and evening his father prayed. He had told Caleb that God—who was so perfect that His name could never be mentioned—knew everything, not only what they said and did, but also everything that was in their hearts. So Caleb decided that he couldn't talk to God either, for the same reason that he couldn't tell his father. He was too angry and ashamed.

It was a terrible day, during which Caleb grew more sullen and angry. Every now and then he had longed to rush to his father and confess, but each time something held him back—the hope that the ewe might return; the fear of his father's anger.

When darkness came and Asher counted each sheep into the fold, he immediately knew that the brown ewe was missing. Caleb wished the ground could swallow him up just then, but it didn't.

With hanging head, he angrily cried, "It wasn't my fault. I only stopped watching her for a moment."

"Was it my fault?" said the shepherd. "Was it Curly's fault, silly thing that she is, and yet trusting us to protect her?"

Caleb couldn't answer. The way his father said these words filled him with pain. He had trusted Caleb, in the same way Curly trusted men to take care of her. He chewed his lips, and hated Curly more than ever.

"You must go and look for her," his father said.

"I will, at first light. I promise," he responded eagerly.

"Tomorrow will be too late. You must find her now."

"But it's dark. I won't be able to see her."

"She'll hear your voice, and you'll hear her's if she's in distress and calling for help."

Caleb was frightened of the dark. "Please don't make me go," he pleaded.

But his father went on, "Look among the thorn bushes, look among the rocks, and the dips in the ground. She'll have the lamb with her. You've got your sling to protect you, as well as our God. You'll never be a good shepherd until you learn to care about the sheep more than you care about yourself."

With these words ringing in his ears and hurting in his heart, Caleb took a thin barley loaf for his supper and his father's cloak to keep him warm, and set out.

At first he had hurried, tripping over the cloak until he wrapped its ends round his shoulders. But soon he was tired, and could hardly keep his eyes open and his legs moving.

The moon, bright and full, threw up all kinds of shadows round about him. Thorn bushes became giant, clawing fingers; rocks became vast caverns. Everything looked big and strange, nothing like the daytime place of grazing, and Caleb was afraid.

Several times Caleb called Curly's name at the top of his voice, listening hopefully for a reply. None came, and soon even his voice in that wilderness began to frighten him.

Then he came to the thorn tree, where he sat down to eat his bread. He was so tired and cold that he thought he would just stay there for a little while to rest and get warm. While he ate, desert noises sounded in his ears—whisperings, scratchings, little mice running hither and thither, scorpions, bigger creatures, perhaps....

Caleb shivered. His heart beat so fast that it sounded as loud in his ears as the night noises all around him. What about evil spirits? Surely they could see him here and would try to devour him?

He jumped up and pulled the broken branches up all around him, far too frightened now to go any further. Snakes, jackals, lions . . . his head was full of horrible imaginings.

He remembered his father's words, "You have our God to protect you," and there was comfort in the thought that God, whose name could never be spoken, was indeed watching him right now and understood his fears.

Caleb pulled his father's cloak right over his head and curled up as close to the trunk of the thorn tree as he could. And there he remained until the black raven woke him with his strident cry.

Caleb was wide awake now and dread made his heart beat fast as he recalled how often he had seen black birds like this one perched on the flank of a dead animal, tearing at its rotting flesh. Ravens were scavengers.

"They have their place," his father had said, when Caleb had first exclaimed in disgust and horror at the sight. "They keep the pastures clean."

But Asher didn't like ravens, either. Too many times they attacked lambing ewes when they were helpless, even killing the lambs before they first felt ground under their hooves. Suppose this had happened to Curly and her lamb? Caleb shivered, but now, the sooner he found out, the better.

He was hungry but he'd already eaten all the bread, so there was no need to waste time on breakfast. Before setting out again he repeated the prayers his father said each morning, then added a special one of his own.

"Please help me find Curly quickly. Please let her be all right."

With this single comfort, and his father's cloak pulled round his shoulders, he set off towards a rocky hillside where thorn bushes and wild flowers almost glittered in the sun. It was a good spot for a lambing ewe seeking a secret place to give birth. Surely she must be there.

The raven gave a cry, spread his powerful wings, and flapped ahead of him, his shadow falling over

Caleb as he passed. He reached the hilly place before Caleb and perched on a rock, where he began to preen his feathers and clean his beak. The raven was the only living thing that Caleb saw and his heart sank, in spite of his prayer. Was God telling him through this raven that he had come too late?

Soon he knew the answer. Clambering over the rocks, then following a line of stale sheep droppings, a woolly brown heap on the ground suddenly hit his gaze. This was Curly and she was dead. Flies were gathered thickly where other creatures had already feasted, and Caleb was stopped in his tracks.

Death was frightening. He could never get used to it, although it was about him all the time in one way or another—in the stories his father told; in the things the village women said and whispered about; in the flock itself, where sheep would die for all sorts of silly reasons and usually so suddenly.

This was the worst thing about death, its suddenness, pouncing like a beast of prey in the dark, completely without pity. Curly's mangled carcass brought it all home to him anew, and the weight of it was his, because he hadn't looked after her.

What about the lamb? Had some jackal or lion carried it off? Had it been completely devoured already? Reluctantly Caleb looked about, not wanting to find another corpse but expecting nothing else.

Caleb's instinct was to run back to his father as fast as he could. He didn't care how angry he would be, just as long as he himself could be away from that horrible sight. Instead he ran towards the raven, which was still watching him, hands searching for his sling and a stone.

"Go away," he yelled. "You've already had your fill!"

The raven rose up with a great flapping of wings and a startled cry. Just as Caleb was about to take aim at him, he heard another cry, quite different from the raven's, which stopped him short. It was the bleat of a lamb, weak and frail, but surely the cry of a lamb in need!

Where had it come from? Where was the lamb? Caleb listened impatiently. "Where are you?" he called.

There was another bleat, somewhere to his right, where the rocky ground gave way abruptly to a sheer drop of about ten feet, at the bottom of which grew a tangled thicket of flowering thorns, full of spikes.

As Caleb looked down, another bleat, stronger than the last, drew his gaze, and there was the lamb, in among that tangle, somehow so caught that he could not move, except for his head and tail that waggled excitedly at the sight of Caleb.

He must have fallen over the edge, Caleb decided, and perhaps Curly had stood on this spot for ages, bleating out a distress that only the predators heard.... It was impossible to know just what had happened but one thing was sure. The thorns that had imprisoned the lamb had also saved his life.

With rising excitement, Caleb found his way down to the lower level, but reaching the lamb wasn't going to be easy. He hacked at the branches with his knife and picked up a stone to break off the spikes which tore at his jacket, wishing he had his father's big club for this work. Soon he was very hot.

The lamb struggled frantically, expecting the worst,

not knowing that Caleb had come to save him. His bleats were loud and filled with fear.

He was a beautiful lamb, absolutely white except for a darker smudge round his nose and the patches of red on the woolly skin where thorns had pierced him. There weren't many white lambs in the flock and they were always precious. The wool fetched a better price than colored wool. Perhaps his father would be less angry when he saw this white lamb.

"Stop struggling," he cried, as the lamb's own efforts got him more and more entangled and hurt. "Can't you see I'm trying to help you? You'll die if you stay here."

The lamb did stop struggling after a while, not because he was no longer frightened but because he was too exhausted. Long before Caleb was able to reach and free him—gasping with pain as his own hands were torn by the thorns that held the lamb prisoner— he had shut his eyes and given up the fight.

He opened his eyes again with a start and a bleat of fear as he felt Caleb's hands round him, and to the boy's amazement, put up a last-ditch fight of surprising courage. In the end Caleb had to pull him free by his front legs while the lamb bleated through wide open mouth, still trying to kick himself free. Even as he sat on the ground and pulled the little creature to him, wanting to reassure him with the warmth of his body and his cradling arms, the lamb strained stiffly against him.

Caleb could feel its heart beating wildly against his own. What fright was in that pounding heart!

"Quiet, quiet," he murmured. "I'm not going to

hurt you," and his sore hands caressed the little body instinctively, wanting to bring him peace.

The lamb gave up struggling. Perhaps Caleb's hands reminded him of the first comfort he had ever received, when his mother had nuzzled and prodded him and licked him clean, bringing warmth to his body and taking darkness from his eyes.

Violent pangs of hunger overwhelmed him and he began prodding Caleb's body with his nose, looking for somewhere to suck. Caleb gave the lamb two fingers and the lamb clung fiercely to them, butting his hard little head against Caleb's chest.

Soon he let out a blurt of frustrated rage. There was no milk in Caleb's fingers. This last seemed just too much for him. He doubled onto his knees and gave up trying. His half cold little body, stained with blood, sprawled against Caleb, no longer fearing, no longer caring.

The dark nostrils were as closed as his eyes, as if no longer caring to breathe. The long tail lay still and lifeless and, as Caleb looked at him, a rush of pain swept into his heart such as he had never felt before. This was love, though he didn't know it then.

All Caleb knew then was that this pain prompted him to jump to his feet, pull the lamb across his shoulders, and set off for his father's grazing grounds as quickly as he could. He forgot his own aches, his own pains, his own fears, filled with determination to keep this lamb alive in spite of all the odds.

The sun was high overhead now, and even the spring sun had a lot of heat in it. It beat down on the lone figure of Caleb with the lamb across his shoulders,

18

and more than once Caleb was tempted to set down his load to rest. Only that fierce pain in his heart kept him from this temptation. He must get back, or the lamb would die.

Caleb's heart suddenly lifted with hope as the first sheep came into sight, and then his father, not far away, overseeing them all. He called out and his father answered and immediately came towards him.

He took the lamb from Caleb's shoulders and cradled it in his arms. There were no words of reproach, no demands for explanation. The shepherd could almost tell the story for himself from Caleb's torn clothes and the deep scratches on his arms and hands.

Asher said, "He's so weak there's not much hope for him. If he's got the will, he'll live. If he hasn't, he'll be dead by nightfall."

Although Caleb's whole body ached from the effort of carrying the lamb so far, there was still much more to be done. Somehow the lamb had to be fed but he was too weak now to be put to one of the ewes.

Caleb's father brought him some milk in a bowl. "Try feeding him yourself," he said. "Dip your fingers in the milk and put them in the lamb's mouth. Keep trying, till he understands. Don't give up, even though he has."

Caleb thought he would enjoy this task, but he was tired and he soon began to grow angry. It looked as though the lamb that had been so brave in the thicket had lost the will to live. The warm, sweet milk had no effect on him.

"Come on, come on," Caleb shouted at him because he wouldn't drink, wouldn't even open his eyes.

Had he worked so much for nothing? He might just as well have left the lamb to die in the thicket.

In his impatience, he pulled open the side of the lamb's lips and tried to force some milk into his mouth. The lamb shook his head. Most of the milk just soaked through Caleb's tunic and trickled down his legs. But some of it must have reached his throat because suddenly the lamb made a choking, gulping sort of sound which forced him to open his mouth.

Hastily Caleb tipped some more milk into the lamb's mouth, letting it run down his fingers which kept the jaws apart. Then something seemed to happen to the lamb's legs as he pushed himself up with a half kick of protest, wakening a flicker of life once more.

Caleb felt the almost lifeless tongue take feeble hold of his fingers and with a grin of joy he let the milk drip, drip, drip onto them into the lamb's mouth.

Soon the bowl was empty. Not much of its contents had reached the lamb's stomach, but it was a start. Several more times Asher brought milk for the lamb and each time he took it more willingly before falling back into deathlike slumber.

Caleb didn't need to be told to stay by the lamb and watch him. Nothing would have taken him from that place. He watched the lamb's flank heave in short, sharp gasps, each moment wondering if this breath was the last, but by nightfall the lamb was on all fours and butting Caleb with an excited bleat when the smell of milk in the bowl reached his nostrils.

He wasn't strong. He staggered and would have fallen, had Caleb not kept him steady, but the milk went down, giving hope to Caleb's anxious heart.

That night the boy and the lamb slept together, under the same goatskin blanket, and perhaps the lamb thought Caleb was his mother because he was no longer afraid.

~3~

Over supper that night Caleb told his father the full story about Curly and the lamb. He didn't tell how scared he had been, or how he had slept under the thorn tree. Perhaps his father knew, anyway.

Caleb knew that his father had sent him out deliberately, not so much as a punishment but as a lesson to be learned. The life of a shepherd was a hard one. Many months were spent away from home, away from the village, out in the desert and mountains, seeking grazing for the sheep.

"If you don't get hard from the beginning," Caleb's father told him, "you won't survive."

"I don't want to be a shepherd," Caleb had complained very early, because he had hardly been weaned from his mother before his father took him off to the pastures, when he was only about five years old.

He had clung to his mother, but she had pushed him away, telling him he must go. It wasn't safe for a boy child to be in the village, especially a boy as strong and handsome as Caleb. The Egyptian masters were jealous of Hebrew boy children, she told him. They might kill him, or take him away to be a slave. It was better to be out of sight, safe among the sheep, where no harm could befall him except the natural things that God might allow.

Caleb had been too young then to understand these things. The abrupt separation from mother and home filled him with resentment. His sisters were able to stay. Nobody wanted to kill them! He had been cherished and spoiled and allowed his own way in most things, then suddenly he was thrust from easy childhood into the rigors of a nomadic life.

At that time Caleb hardly knew his father, Asher the shepherd. He hadn't wanted to go off with him—a black-bearded stranger who dressed in goatskins and smelled like the animals he lived among, and hardly knew how to talk to so small a child.

Several years had passed since then and now Caleb was used to sleeping on the ground, with his feet near the fire. He was used to walking for miles each day, at a sheep's pace. He had learned many things in that time, and especially he had learned to love his father and almost to forget his mother and sisters—except in a very deep and special way which he kept in a silent place in his heart.

At night, when the sheep were safely in the fold— which was sometimes a place Asher had built with his own hands from rocks in the desert, topped with thorn branches, and sometimes a natural cave which had sheltered sheep for years—Asher would make a fire and prepare their food.

After they had eaten, he would talk to Caleb and tell him all the things he knew about the stars and the sky and the flowers and the wild animals, and Caleb listened and learned.

He talked about the sheep, too, but Caleb still hated the sheep because they had taken him away from home, and kept him away from home. Although he learned many things about them, his father could not make him love them or take an interest in them, because love is a natural thing that cannot be forced.

What Caleb liked best was when his father told him stories about their own people. They were exciting stories, but even though these people had been shepherds themselves—owners of great herds of cattle, as well as sheep and goats and donkeys and camels, much richer than Asher—this still didn't make Caleb want to be a shepherd.

That night, when Caleb told his father the details of how he had saved the lamb from the thorn bush, enjoying the telling the more because the lamb was snuggled against him, fast asleep, his father said, "In the story of Isaac, the lamb was caught in a thorn bush."

Caleb pretended he couldn't remember the story, because he wanted to hear it again, and his father pretended to believe him because he liked telling it. So, while the flames of the fire flickered and gradually died down into glowing ashes, and the stars grew brighter overhead, Asher told Caleb again how their father Abraham had taken his son, Isaac, to be sacrificed because this was what God had commanded him to do.

When Caleb first heard about his father Abraham he had really believed that Abraham was somehow his father, as well as Asher. But then the shepherd explained that Abraham was the father of all the Hebrew people—but that was another story.

Abraham's wife, Sarah, had no children and this was a great sorrow to them. Abraham had so many cattle and sheep and donkeys and yet he had no son who could inherit these things. Then, when both he and Sarah were past dreaming about having a son, Isaac was born to them.

Isaac was a special gift from God, who had promised Abraham that he would be the father of many nations. Caleb loved this part of the story. His father always told it the same way.

"God said to Abraham—Come out of your tent and look at the stars. See if you can count them. You will have more children than there are stars in the sky."

And Caleb would look up at the stars. He couldn't count them. He could still count only as far as the fingers on both hands, and there were many, many times that number of stars in the blackness over his head. Sometimes, when he thought he had seen them all, he would suddenly find another he hadn't noticed, then another, and another.

It took his breath away at times, just to look at the stars. They were so beautiful, the way they shone and sometimes seemed to blink. And God had promised Abraham that his children would be like the stars.

It made Caleb's heart warm when he knew that he was one of the children God had promised to Abraham. He smiled to himself, then grinned at his father when he saw how he looked at him. He knew his father was pleased to be one of Abraham's children, too.

Sometimes they both looked up at the stars for a long time and Asher would point out the important ones, but tonight Caleb wanted to hear about the lamb, so he urged his father, "Go on. Tell what happened next."

Next was when Isaac was a young man. Abraham loved him dearly because he was a good son, and a blessing from God. But then one day God told Abraham to take Isaac to a mountain. When they reached the mountain Abraham had to kill Isaac and offer him to God as a sacrifice.

This was the part of the story Caleb couldn't understand, even though he knew how the story ended. His father said, "God wanted to know if Abraham trusted him," but still Caleb found it very hard.

He always imagined himself as Isaac, remembering when his father had come one day to take him away from home, and he had cried and clung to his mother and said, "I don't want to go. I don't want to go."

But Isaac had obediently gone with his father and had even carried the firewood which would burn him while Abraham carried the knife and the fire itself. Abraham hadn't told Isaac where they were going, or why. He just said they were going to worship God in the mountain, but when Isaac saw the wood and the knife and the fire he knew they were going to make a sacrifice.

He said to his father, "We've brought the fire and the wood, but where is the lamb for the burnt offering?"

Abraham answered, "God Himself will provide the lamb for the sacrifice, my son."

At this point in the story Caleb's heart always began to beat fast. If he'd been Isaac he would have wanted to run away. He himself knew enough about sheep to realize that a lamb on its own in the wilderness wouldn't survive long enough for Abraham to find it alive, and you couldn't offer to God a lamb that had been half eaten by ravens or wolves.

There wouldn't be any lamb in the mountain. Abraham didn't expect to find a lamb. He was going to kill his son.

Then Abraham found some stones and built an altar, and when the wood was in place, ready to be kindled, Isaac himself knew what must happen next. There was no lamb, only himself, and he obediently laid himself down on the altar, waiting for his father to kill him.

Caleb's heart burned. Suppose God told his own father to kill him one day? Would he do it? Would Caleb be obedient like Isaac and let him? He felt a trembling all through his body. This God was a strange God, impossible to understand.

Then, just when Abraham was going to kill his son with the knife, still trusting God, he heard an angel call out to him.

"Abraham, Abraham, don't touch the boy. Don't harm him. Now I know that you trust God because you are ready to give up your son, your only son."

And when Abraham looked up he saw a lamb caught in a thicket by its horns. It hadn't been there before, or he would have seen it. God had put the lamb there so that Isaac would not have to die. So Abraham cut the lamb free from the thorns and sacrificed it instead of his son.

"And Abraham called that place The Lord will Provide," finished Asher, "because our God always provides for us when we trust Him."

Caleb wondered about the lamb that God had put in the thicket to die instead of Isaac. It wouldn't have been a little lamb, like the one curled up against him now, because it had horns. His little lamb didn't have horns yet. He had been caught by his legs and his woolly skin and there were deep gashes which his father had covered with oil where the thorns had torn him.

It was a strange and exciting story, but this was the first time that Caleb found himself thinking about the lamb that God had provided to save someone's life. What did it mean?

His father said God never did anything without a purpose and that it was important just to trust God because you could never understand Him.

Later, when he was trying to sleep but couldn't, because his mind kept going over all the things of that day—and the lamb under the goatskin with him was making snorting noises, and now and again pushing against him—it seemed to Caleb that God had provided this lamb for him because he had nothing of his own.

He smiled to himself because, with the lamb curled close beside him, he felt warm and satisfied. That new feeling in his heart was still there, and it was a good feeling.

~4~

The lamb survived the night and was on all fours in the morning, bleating out his hunger. Caleb's father found a sheep with a full udder and kept her still so that the lamb could suck and drink his fill. He was strong enough to do that now, but his strength was finished by the time his belly was full.

When Asher let the ewe go, the lamb made no effort to run after her. He didn't seem to recognize that he belonged to the flock. He didn't want her company.

Asher said to Caleb, "Don't raise your hopes yet. It might be days before we can really know if he'll live or not. I've nursed a motherless lamb for a week or more before losing it."

"This one's not going to die," insisted Caleb. "I won't let him."

His father was pleased with this reply. He looked into Caleb's earnest dark eyes and said, "Perhaps he will live, then, if you take great care of him."

Caleb did take great care of him. He still had to watch over the sheep his father had put in his charge. Remembering how Curly had wandered off so quickly, he refused to allow his attention to be distracted by lizards or beetles or strange marks in the dust. He even tried not to let the lamb distract him too much, though this was more difficult.

While the sheep grazed, he sat in a place where he could see them easily enough and the lamb slept beside him. Caleb thought he slept far too much. He saw the other lambs frolicking with each other, playing games, and he wanted his lamb to do the same.

The shepherd had looked at his wounds again. They weren't deep and would heal quickly. He had run his knowing hands over the whole of that lanky body, feeling the bones, and he said to Caleb, "He'll be a good lamb, if he lives."

Caleb, on his own, did as he had seen his father do. He felt the long, strong leg bones; the solidness of the shoulder; the straightness of the back. And as he went all over the lamb like this, there was that feeling again inside him that made his heart swell.

Several times that day the lamb was put to one of the ewes to drink his fill, and by nightfall he certainly seemed a good deal stronger and more willing to stay on his legs.

"Perhaps he'll be all right," said Asher. "Tomorrow we'll see if one of the ewes will accept him, and then we'll be able to let him run with the flock."

Caleb had mixed feelings about this. He wanted the lamb to be strong. He wanted him to live. He knew that it was right for the lamb to be among the others, but...once he was among the others, then he would not be Caleb's lamb any more. He'd become just one of the flock and if more white lambs were born then Caleb might not be able to tell his lamb apart from the others.

He was silent after his father spoke, not daring to contradict him, yet longing so much to say what was in his heart. But Asher noticed. His sharp eyes missed nothing, whether he was watching sheep or people.

"What's the matter?" he asked.

"I want him to be my lamb," mumbled Caleb, hardly daring to look at his father and hardly daring to say the next words. "Can't I keep him and look after him?"

"It's hard work, rearing a lamb yourself. You have enough to do with the work I give you, and you do it badly. If your mind is on one particular lamb all the time you'll be forgetting the others, and making things more difficult for me."

"I won't. I promise I won't. I'll care more, really I will."

"Why this sudden change?" asked Asher. "Only two days ago you were full of resentment."

His words struck deep into Caleb's heart. He knew how true they were, and yet he knew, too, that they weren't true any more. These hours with the lamb had made him feel so different, but how could he explain this to his father? He had never talked about himself before, about his feelings, and these were very deep feelings, difficult to explain.

Perhaps his very silence was full of explanation. Perhaps the feelings were written on his face and Asher could see them in the firelight.

Suddenly he said, "Very well. The lamb is yours. If you look after him well he'll grow into a fine ram."

Caleb stared at his father in astonishment, hardly able to believe what he heard. He knew just how much each sheep meant to his father. He wouldn't lightly give away a lamb. The sheep were like children to him. In exchange for their wool and milk, he gave them every hour of his life. And when one died, or had to be killed because it was sick beyond cure and in pain, it was a very real loss to him.

"Do you mean he'll really be mine, or just to look after till he's strong?" Caleb asked, wanting to be sure.

Thoughtfully Asher replied, "Perhaps the Lord provided him, like the Isaac lamb, to teach you to care about the sheep. You can't care about something you don't love, and it's been plain to me that you don't love the sheep.

"When you were little, I understood. I thought you would grow to love them as time went by. But all I've seen is that you dislike them more and more. You're impatient with them. You try to drive them, rather than lead them. You don't notice when one is sick or lame. You don't notice when one is missing. You don't know one from another."

Caleb's heart cringed as his father spoke. All these things were true. The strange thing was that, just a short while ago, these words would have made him angry. He might not have spoken aloud his resentment, but in his heart he would have thought, "So what? I don't want to be a shepherd so why should I care?"

But this little lamb had changed his heart.

"I will care about him," he cried. "I do love him. I do want him to be mine."

Asher went on, "If I see that you care, if you rear this lamb well, then next year I'll let you choose another from the flock. It would be good for you to have sheep of your own. The hired hand never cares about the sheep as much as the shepherd. Perhaps this is where I have been wrong. Perhaps from the beginning I should have given you a lamb of your own to care for."

He looked keenly at Caleb and went on, "You wouldn't have let Curly stray if she had belonged to you. But perhaps it was the Lord's will, so that He could put this lamb into your hands."

Even such sobering words could not alter Caleb's excitement. "And is he really mine? Can I do what I like with him?"

Asher thought for a moment before replying, "Yes, but remember—when you love something, you have to think of its needs before your own. Loving means giving. So it won't be a question of doing what you like, but doing what is right for the lamb. Remember that and you'll do the right thing."

"What shall I call him?" said Caleb, his heart so full that he had to grasp at something simpler.

His father said, "He's your lamb. You must choose his name."

Caleb looked at his lamb, even now asleep with his head across the boy's thigh, and he thought of all the names his father gave to the sheep. They weren't very exciting, and they often came from things he said about them.

If one of them was a straggler, by the time he'd called out, "Come on, lazy-bones," three or four times that sheep became known as Lazy-Bones till the end of her life, even though afterwards she might change her ways.

There was one he called Princess because he said she was the most beautiful sheep in the flock, with deer-like eyes, fawn coloring, and as perfect a shape as a sheep can have.

In the end, because the thought was constantly in his mind, Caleb said, "Do you think I could call him

Isaac, because of Isaac's lamb? Do you think that's a good name for him?"

"It's a good name," agreed Asher. "According to tradition, Isaac was given his name because it means 'he laughs' and his mother, Sarah, said this son would bring her laughter. Perhaps this lamb will bring you laughter, too."

The lamb did bring laughter to Caleb's life, just as soon as he was strong enough to become aware of the world around him. Sweet milk and warm sun poured strength into him, day after day, and he felt it first in his lanky legs.

It was comical to see him trying out movements which should have come easily to him only a few hours after birth and yet which, several days later, he wasn't really sure of.

Even very young lambs frolicked and skipped and jumped without losing their balance. But Isaac had a clumsiness about him, due to his weakness, which had him tumbling on his nose or collapsing in a heap of tangled legs, and made Caleb roll up with laughter.

When the lamb heard Caleb's laughter, he stared at him with such puzzlement, legs splayed apart, still uncertain, that he looked funnier still and made the boy laugh even more. But as his strength grew Caleb had no cause to laugh, except for joy, because Isaac became as sure-footed and well-balanced as any lamb in the flock.

Joyful laughter is the best kind and Asher was glad to hear this joy in his son's voice. In their years together he hadn't heard it often. There wasn't a great deal to laugh about in their existence. So it did the shepherd's heart good to hear his son, and to see the joy that was in him because the lamb was his.

Caleb decided that it was right for the lamb to return to the flock if a ewe could be persuaded to foster him. As he thought over his father's words about the meaning of love he knew it would be wrong to keep Isaac apart from his own kind. This was his first hard decision and he had to pray first of all, "Please, Lord, help me to do the right thing," before he could make up his mind.

It wasn't necessary any more to hold little Isaac's muzzle to the teat. He was eager now to get the milk for himself, and Caleb laughed with delight to see how his little hooves stamped and his long tail wagged with excitement because the milk wouldn't come fast enough.

The ewe seemed willing to accept him, though she had a lamb of her own, bigger than Isaac. While the white lamb suckled on one side, her own spotted youngling suckled on the other, and, although it pained his heart, Caleb was willing to allow Isaac to follow his foster-mother and her youngster back to the flock.

However, Isaac didn't seem to realize that he was meant to be part of the flock. He was eager enough to suckle but once he'd had his fill he turned to Caleb for company, determined to follow him—and only him—everywhere.

Caleb, of course, was thrilled. He felt it was his duty to try to get Isaac into the flock again—and once even left him among the sheep, hoping for better results. But after staring at them all with pricked ears and puzzled eyes, Isaac opened wide his mouth and bleated anxiously for the only "mother" he was really attached to.

"You're supposed to stay with the others," Caleb scolded him, when he came to his rescue—seeing him so frightened and alone—but there was joy in his voice that he couldn't disguise.

When he told his father how he had tried to encourage Isaac to become part of the flock, Asher was amused by Caleb's triumphant finish, "But he wants to stay with me. He can stay with me, can't he?"

"I don't see how you're going to stop him," laughed the shepherd. "Whether you like it or not, that lamb's adopted you. But don't let him interfere with your work."

~5~

Spring was the very best time of year, when all the desert flowers burst into life and grazing was plentiful everywhere. The sheep hardly needed to move in order to fill their bellies, as they grazed hock deep amid wild flowers of every color, and there was a great contentment among them.

The sun, though strong, had not reached its summer intensity, when the flowers would fade and every bit of grass and shade would be jostled over.

Almost as if aware that this good time could not last, the flock kept its head down all day long, nibbling away at the juicy stems and grasses. And the lambs put their heads down and copied their mothers, though not so seriously because milk was still their main diet.

As Caleb's lamb grew stronger and fitter he started to look towards the flock, as well as to the boy, for companionship. The bleating of the other lambs attracted him, though he was deaf to the calls of the older sheep. He was as eager as any youngster seeing children of his own age, wanting to mix and play with them.

Caleb was pleased when Isaac began joining the games of the other lambs, and he laughed and cheered him on in his mock battles. A favorite game was when one of them found a little mound on which he could stand and, with loud bleats, proclaimed that this bit of territory belonged only to him.

Isaac loved this game in particular, as if he was

planning from the very beginning to be boss of the flock one day. He would rush up every mound, clamber up every outcrop of rocks, and stand there, head lowered, fiercely protecting what he had claimed for himself. Little horn buds were already beginning to sprout and Isaac shook his head proudly, already knowing how he would use these horns one day.

If another lamb tried to take the mound from him, they would go round and round, head flat against head, eyes almost touching, each one pushing with all his might until one gave way or grew bored with the game, or heard his mother calling.

When tiredness overtook him, as it overtook all the lambs sooner or later, Isaac would find his way back to Caleb and fall asleep somewhere near him, rather than stay among his fellows. He knew now who his foster-mother was and would search her out for himself when he was hungry, but he felt no need of her for anything else, always coming back to Caleb.

Isaac grew rapidly and, as Caleb's father had already foreseen, was undoubtedly the handsomest male lamb of that spring. Although he had started so badly, there was no reminder now of those first feeble days. He was round and fat and tall, and his wool was as white as the snow Caleb saw on the mountain tops in winter.

There were other white lambs but none as white as Isaac. Most of them had a bit of brown on their faces, or black on their knees, or spots on their rumps, but Isaac was pure white from nose to tail.

Never before had Caleb noticed these differences between one lamb and another, and as he talked to his father about them—always comparing the other lambs unfavorably with his own—Asher smiled and said with approval, "I knew that lamb would make a shepherd of you."

Caleb felt very proud.

As he compared his lamb with the rest, and saw how each one was different—not only because their markings were different but because their faces and characters were different, too—he suddenly understood how his father knew which ones to keep a special eye on and which ones he could leave alone.

Some looked mean, some looked silly, some looked thoughtful; some had haughty faces; some were very humble. You could tell which ones were going to be the troublemakers, which ones were likely to get lost, which ones would want to go their own way.

Knowing the sheep made the shepherd's job easier, and when Caleb discovered this, he suddenly wanted to know them all and then find out from his father if he was right in his judgment of them.

Sometimes his father would agree with him, but sometimes he would point to other things that Caleb hadn't yet noticed.

When he said confidently, "That one with the long nose—she looks like a real bossy one," Asher replied, "Yes, she's got a bossy face, but look at her eyes. Shifty. She'll be the boss when she thinks she can get away with it, but she'll run just as soon as she's challenged. Watch, and see for yourself."

Caleb did watch, and the more he watched, the more he discovered for himself and the more there was for him to share with his father.

This sharing was a new joy to Caleb. So often he

had felt his father to be hard and distant with him, caring more about the sheep than about him. But when Caleb started sharing and caring with him, then they became companions as well as father and son.

What a joyful spring it was. Suddenly every day had a purpose to it. Like the lamb himself, every day Caleb discovered new things and grew more confident. There was time to play, too.

One of the hardest things in Caleb's life had been a lack of playmates. At home he had played with his younger sisters. He had been the center of attention in those days because his mother knew just how soon she would have to part with him. But the shepherd had forgotten how a boy's heart longs for someone to wrestle with, someone to share things with, someone to challenge.

Now he had the lamb in whose bouncy legs and healthy bones were the same longings to be found in Caleb—a desire to run and jump and chase and fight and pretend.

Caleb and Isaac had great games together, chasing each other, wrestling with each other, the lamb trying out his budding horns against Caleb and Caleb straining every muscle to catch Isaac when he refused to be caught. Even though Isaac couldn't laugh as Caleb laughed, in his bleats and his stampings and his wagging tail there was surely as much joy as in Caleb's laughter.

Caleb played with his lamb as he might have played with the boys in his village, had there been boys there to play with. But those were hard days for the Hebrew people, and boys didn't play in the streets. By the time they were Caleb's age most of them were at work under Egyptian masters, unless they had herdsmen fathers who could take them off to the pastures and keep them hidden.

It was through his father's prayers that Caleb came to know that their people were kept in the land of Egypt against their will. Only through his prayers did he know that God had promised one day to remember them and take them out of this land of slavery and set them free.

When Caleb asked about these things, Asher explained how Joseph had been sold as a slave to the Egyptians many, many generations ago.

"But because God loved him, he made him a great man, much loved by the Pharaoh."

Caleb was interested in Joseph because he was the grandson of Isaac, and from being a slave had become the most important man in all the land. Joseph used to dream and God would show him what his dreams meant. God also gave him the power to explain the dreams of other people, and Joseph saved Egypt from terrible famine because of this gift to understand dreams. And then Joseph's own family—his father and brothers—came to Egypt and the Pharaoh loved them because he loved Joseph.

"But since those days the Egyptians have grown jealous of us because they see that our God keeps His promises and makes us a strong people, while the idols they worship do nothing."

"What will happen when we are free?" Caleb wondered.

"We'll be able to go home whenever we want to.

We won't have to stay away from your mother and sisters and never know how they are. And they won't have to be afraid for us, that we might one day be killed by the Egyptians."

And Asher explained how boy children had to be hidden from the Egyptians because Pharaoh had given the order that all boy children be put to death at birth.

"Is that why I'm here with you, and why we hardly ever go home?" said Caleb, understanding at last.

"It is."

"I'm glad I'm here with you," said Caleb, and for the first time he really meant it, thanks to the Isaac lamb.

Once the lambing was over, and the young lambs were strong enough to be kept on the move, Asher led his flock to the shearing place. This was a communal fold to which the shepherds came from many places at the same time of year. They helped each other with the shearing; they exchanged rams and ewes to get fresh blood for their flocks and, as much as anything else, they exchanged news.

Shearing was always an exciting time, even for Caleb. He would meet other boys like himself and, once the shyness was broken down, they would have stories to tell, games to play, experiences to share— just like their fathers and uncles.

This year Caleb wanted to boast to the other boys about his lamb. He had never had anything to boast about before.

The boys copied their fathers. They judged Isaac by running their hands over him to feel his flesh and bones. They stood back to examine his overall appearance. They ran their fingers through the growing wool. And, like their fathers, they nodded their heads wisely and said that Isaac was a fine lamb—so white, so strong, so clean of any blemish. Caleb was satisfied.

Shearing was a noisy time, a hubbub of fear, complaint, and confusion as each animal was dealt with— mothers separated from younglings and the lambs not recognizing them when they were together again, so different did they look. Released from the heavy weight of wool, the adults hardly seemed to know themselves. They jumped and skittered about and startled their own lambs who were used to their mothers being much more sedate.

Caleb's lamb didn't recognize his foster-mother without her fleece and there was a great exchange of bleats and baas before at last he would go to her to fill his hungry belly, sure of a welcome rather than a kick.

At the end of each day everyone was tired. Backs ached, heads ached from the noise, but weariness was soon forgotten as the shepherds came together to share the evening meal and to praise their God—that mysterious God who meant so much to them and yet whom Caleb hardly understood.

This shearing time their praises were louder than Caleb ever remembered them being before. In other years their groanings were louder than their praises as they remembered grievances and ill-treatment meted out to them by the Egyptians generation after generation—sons murdered, brothers worked to death, wives and mothers full of sorrow.

But this shearing time they praised God loudly because news had come to them of a messenger sent to Pharaoh by God Himself. At last the Lord had heard their prayers. At last He had answered them through this man who had come to demand in God's name that His people be set free.

Caleb knew that God's name could never be spoken, but this man had been given a name by God Himself that he could use, a name as mysterious as God Himself—I am who I am.

Caleb heard the shepherds say that this man's name was Moses.

~6~

During the night at shearing time the shepherds took it in turn to guard the one entrance to the fold where all the sheep were kept together. There was no gate, only a gap in the wall, and at night the shepherd on duty would sit or stand or lie across that gap. The sheep wouldn't try to jump over him to get out, and a wild animal or a thief couldn't get in unnoticed.

When it was Asher's turn to guard the gate Caleb slept beside him on the ground, and the Isaac lamb slept beside Caleb, just inside the fold. Before he went to sleep Caleb asked his father, "Who is this Moses that everyone is talking about?"

Asher said, "He's a shepherd, as we are, but God has sent him to Pharaoh to tell him to let us go. We're living in exciting days, my son. At long last the Lord has heard us."

"But did God actually come and talk to Moses?" wondered Caleb, not understanding how such a thing could happen.

What did God look like? How would the shepherd, Moses, know it was God?

"He spoke to him from a burning bush in the desert. The bush was full of flames, but it didn't burn up. Not one of the branches was burned."

Caleb tried to imagine such a thing but couldn't.

"And will Pharaoh listen to God?" he asked. "Will he let us go?"

"Yes," said Asher. "He'll listen. Everyone must listen to God."

"And when shall we go?" asked Caleb.

"I don't know the time, but it will be just as soon as Pharaoh knows that the Lord is God, stronger than his gods, stronger than his army, stronger than his people."

"Will that take long?"

"Perhaps. Pharaoh has a heart of stone."

"And where will we go?"

"To a new land the Lord has prepared for us, better than this one." Asher spoke with absolute certainty.

"Will the sheep come with us?" Caleb wanted to know.

"Surely they will."

"And my lamb, Isaac—he'll come, too?"

"Of course. When we are a free people there'll be an even greater need for sheep and shepherds."

"And my mother and sisters will come, won't they?"

"Yes, and we'll live together without fear. This very winter we'll go home to them. Perhaps we'll never have to be separated again. We'll have a new home in a new place, thanks to our God who has answered our prayers."

Caleb fell asleep, unable to think of any more questions. The answers his father had given him, the excitement that was among all the shepherds, filled his head and heart so much that everything spilled over into dreams.

He dreamt he was a shepherd like his father, tall and black-bearded, and with a flock that was all his own. And the Isaac lamb was father of all the flock. Yet somehow in his dream the lamb hadn't grown. He was still a baby, as he was in real life, still suckling from his foster-mother, still gambolling and battling and pretending to be a fierce old ram. Dreams were like that. They made sense while you were asleep, but not once you woke up.

Caleb told Isaac about his dream—not that the lamb understood. But he rubbed his hard head against Caleb's legs, butting and stamping, and made the boy laugh with joy.

When the shearing was over it was time to take the flocks to the summer pastures. Each day the sun stayed longer in the sky; each day its heat was more intense. The grasses and flowers which had burst out after the spring rains were drying up where they hadn't been eaten. The sheep needed better pastures, and Asher knew where they were.

Days of slow trekking followed, always at a pace the sheep could manage. When a lamb was tired or footsore Asher would carry it across his shoulders. Caleb was still not strong enough to do that, for the lambs were big now, but he had his own load—the cooking pot and the bag of barley flour—which grew heavier and heavier as the sun's rays poured down endlessly upon him.

At noon they would seek a shady place to rest. All the sheep would crowd together under a wide-spreading tree, or in the shade of an outcrop of rocks, wherever they could escape the sun, however patchy the shade might be. Often Asher would drape his cloak over his staff like a tent when there was no other shade to be found.

In the morning, before the sun was high, Asher

would pour oil on to each sheep's head, to keep it from getting sunstroke, and Caleb helped him. It was important not to overlook any. A long day in the sun could kill a sheep as much as a man, and the sheep had no covering for their heads as Caleb and his father had.

The summer months were the hardest, with little grazing and even less water. The sun, heat and dust made the sheep restless. They were unable to lie down and sleep because they were hungry. Even Caleb's lamb would spend hours away from the boy, looking for something to nibble.

If Caleb or Asher saw a leafy tree, they would reach up with a staff to shake down the leaves and the sheep would quickly gather round. They hardly took their eyes off the shepherd when they were hungry, trusting Asher to supply them with food. Caleb would save some of the leaves for Isaac's supper and the lamb soon came to expect some sort of tidbit before lying down for the night.

Asher always walked ahead of the flock, eyes constantly searching for things that could harm them, as well as the pasture they needed. When they came to a green place near a desert pool or a stream, before the sheep could graze there it had to be checked for snakes or poisonous weeds.

Horned vipers lived in holes made by burrowing animals and if a sheep happened to graze too close they might dart out and bite its nose, bringing about its death within a few hours. When Asher found a hole that looked like a viper's nest he would pour some oil beside it and set it on fire. The smell and the flame would bring the snake out, and Asher would kill it with his club.

He taught Caleb to recognize the different dangerous plants, reminding him that a careless shepherd could lose a whole flock in a day if he didn't first search new pastures for poisonous herbs.

"Why don't the sheep know they're poisonous?" Caleb wondered.

"They trust us to keep them safe," his father replied.

It was good to find a green place because when the sheep had fed well they would lie down and chew the cud and sleep. Then Asher and Caleb could relax, too, and not have to be watching them every minute. But as the summer days grew longer, it was harder and harder to find pastures not already dried up or stripped of grazing by a flock that had gone that way before them.

"It's time to go to the hills," Asher said one morning, and Caleb's heart sank when he heard these words.

Nothing frightened him more than the dark canyon in the hills through which, twice a year, they had to pass. Even the sheep were terrified of that place. They would huddle together, constantly bleating, their eyes filled with the fear that was in Caleb's own heart.

The canyon was a dark, cold, and narrow place, with sharp drops, overhanging rocks, and deep caves on either side. Who could tell if a lion or a cheetah might be lying on one of those rocks, waiting to drop down without warning across a sheep's back, breaking its neck?

Bands of hungry robbers were known to waylay lonely shepherds as they went through the pass, killing them and stealing the sheep.

Caleb knew his father hated going through the canyon, too, but there was no other way. For Caleb, the worst part was not being able to walk beside his father and perhaps even hold his hand if he was really frightened. Someone had to bring up the rear, to look out for stragglers or a sheep that might slip off the pathway or suddenly go lame. This was Caleb's job and each year he hated it more and more.

His heart would beat hard as he looked up at the overhanging ledges, unable to see the beast of prey that might be there. If one jumped down, what could he do? He had his knife. He had his sling. But one small boy against a lion, a wolf, or even a robber....

His only comfort was the one he shared with the sheep—the sound of his father's voice, and the sound of his club which he would bang against the rock face from time to time.

Asher might be out of sight, far ahead of the tail end of the flock, but he would constantly call out, "Come on, my beauties. Come on, Grey Face. Where are you, Spot?" Things like that. Or he might sing out words of praise to God, which would echo back to sheep and shepherd boy alike, comforting them.

The sound of his voice, the sound of his club, meant everything was all right, that the path was still clear. If he was silent for more than a little while both Caleb and the sheep would begin to get restless. The sheep bleated and pushed against each other, wanting to hurry ahead and not be left behind. There was always the danger that they would push each other off the track—Caleb could still remember with a shudder the time when three of them had tumbled over the sheer rock face and crashed to their deaths far below.

It was his job to keep them calm, but it wasn't easy to speak comforting words when your throat was dry and your heart beating so fast that it made you dizzy. Sometimes it seemed that his tongue was stuck to the roof of his mouth. Words just wouldn't come out. But then the shepherd's club, or his voice, would come echoing back to them again. All was well. They could go on.

This year was better because Caleb had company. The Isaac lamb went along beside him, pressed against his legs. Now and again he bleated like the others, but then he would look up at Caleb and grow quiet.

It was good to have the lamb there, even though neither of them would be any match against a lion. But Caleb somehow felt braver. He wasn't going to let any wild animal or bandit steal his lamb.

He kept a stone in his sling and his eyes on as many places as possible, and the words of comfort he kept offering to Isaac were a comfort to himself, too.

Just beyond the ravine was a spring of water that burst out from the rocks, clear and icy. It ran all over the rock face, forming little pools among the boulders.

Together, Asher and Caleb pulled the boulders aside to make the pools bigger so that the sheep could drink. They wouldn't drink from rushing water, instinctively afraid of it, and they could only suck up long, deep mouthfuls when the water was still.

Caleb enjoyed making pools and dams among the rocks, even though it was hard work. Water was such a scarce thing that it was precious and beautiful. To see it so bountiful; to hear its music as it gushed out of the rock; to be able to feel it tickling his toes and his fingers; all these things were a never ending delight which helped him forget his previous dread.

They stayed beyond the ravine for the rest of the

summer, wandering from one pasture to another, needing to keep alert for beasts of prey. Caleb practiced constantly with his sling, which was a mighty weapon against any enemy. One small stone flying through the air gathered force and weight. It could kill a lion if you hit him between the eyes.

The sling was also useful for keeping the sheep from straying. A pebble hitting the ground just beyond them would bring them scurrying back to the shepherd, however determined they might be to ignore his voice. But you had to be a good shot or you would send them running in the wrong direction, or break a leg if that was where the pebble hit.

As they moved from one pasture to another, Isaac kept close to Caleb. As they went along, whenever Caleb saw a special tuft of grass or wild flowers he pulled them up for Isaac. When the other sheep saw what was happening, some of them would try to push themselves into Isaac's place, hoping to grab the tidbits.

At first Caleb wouldn't give them any, but when he saw how hungry they were, and how patiently and hopefully they kept up with him, he relented just a little. When tidbits were plentiful he did his best to share them equally, but in the end Isaac always got more than the rest.

Asher plucked tidbits for the sheep, too, and the sheep that walked closest to him received the most. Asher never minded which lips snatched up the dainties, but the clever ones soon knew to expect them and jostled with each other and sometimes pushed their heads against the shepherd, reminding him they were there. He knew, of course, and gently told them to be patient.

~7~

All through that summer both Caleb and his lamb grew. Caleb grew taller and stronger and more confident in himself, and Isaac did the same. Caleb was given more responsibility by his father. He was allowed to go first into a pasture to look for snakes or poisonous plants. He was allowed to keep watch on his own while his father slept.

Asher said, "Since you've had that lamb, you're a much better shepherd. You care about him, so you think about his needs, and that makes you think and care about the other sheep, too."

Caleb's heart burned with pride at his father's words, just as it used to burn with shame and anger when he was reminded of his carelessness.

As Isaac grew he became more independent. His foster-mother's milk dried up so, like the rest, most of his time was spent searching for something to eat. But whenever Caleb called him he would instantly lift his head, as if he always had one ear listening.

When he lifted his head, it was always with an eager look as if to say, "Caleb is calling me. What does he want?" And he would come running, to find out. The other sheep would look up, too, to see what was happening, but they seemed to recognize that Isaac and Caleb had a special relationship that didn't include them.

Caleb learned a hard lesson about shepherding

that summer. He knew how much his father loved the sheep and yet one day he seemed to do something very harsh. It concerned one of the sheep that was constantly straying. Time and again she would be brought back, but, as soon as she could, she'd be off again. Sooner or later she would be killed by wild animals, or stolen by another shepherd, and meanwhile she was a constant trial to Asher and Caleb.

Asher said, "We can do one of two things. Either kill her, and at least have a feast ourselves rather than the hyenas or another shepherd, or we can put a stop to her wanderings another way. What do you think?"

Caleb was proud that his father should ask his advice, so he thought very carefully before answering. He was beginning to hate this particular ewe, who made life so wearisome for both of them, but she was young and silly. It was a bit hard to be put to death for that.

"Can't we just stop her from wandering?" he said at last.

"We'll give her one more chance," agreed Asher. "The next time is the last."

Only the very next day she was off again with pricked ears and high raised head, as if searching some pasture that only she knew about just over the next hill, or the next.

Asher brought her back across his shoulders. One leg was dangling, broken.

"How did she do that?" asked Caleb.

"I did it, with my club," said Asher.

Seeing the pained surprise on Caleb's face, he added, "It's not always easy to care for the things you love. Sometimes you have to hurt them to save them from worse things. The broken leg will heal, but she won't wander off again."

The broken-legged ewe caused his father a great deal of trouble. Whenever they were on the move he had to carry her, or leave her behind for the jackals. Yet he picked her up cheerfully and laid her down gently, and brought water to her himself, refreshing her head as well as giving her to drink.

It would have been easier to kill and eat her than do all this for her, and Caleb learned through all that he saw that his father really loved that sheep, even though he had deliberately hurt her. Later Caleb saw that the broken-legged ewe was always the closest to his father when they were on the move, jerking along, nudging at him for tidbits. She had no fear of him and held no grudge against him. It seemed as if she understood.

That summer Caleb and his father met up with other shepherds who had come with their flocks from other places. These men had strange and wonderful things to tell them about the shepherd Moses and his brother Aaron, who was his spokesman. They had called all the chief men of Israel together and told them that God had seen their misery and was going to set them free.

"Not everybody believes it," said the shepherds.

"How can that be?" exclaimed Asher, who trusted God with his life.

"Because when they did miracles, to show that their message was from God, Pharaoh's magic men did the same things. Then Pharaoh just laughed at Moses and Aaron. He has doubled the work of the slaves, so now things are worse than before. The people are groaning and saying, 'A curse on Moses for coming here.'"

Caleb felt frightened. Was their God no more powerful than Pharaoh's magic men?

As if reading his thoughts, one of the shepherds said, "And yet, when Aaron's staff became a snake, and the magicians' staffs also, Aaron's snake swallowed up the other snakes."

"And so will our God swallow up the Egyptians," shouted Asher with a laugh, "whatever Pharaoh's magicians may do."

Caleb was comforted.

"Then, an even stranger thing happened," went on the oldest shepherd, "something we've heard about but not seen, though I would have liked to see such a thing with my own eyes."

"What was it?" cried Caleb, forgetting to be silent in the presence of his elders. Nobody rebuked him. Asher was as eager to hear as this man was to tell. "With the same staff that became a snake, Moses touched the waters of the great river and they turned to blood."

His brother added, "They say that everywhere in Egypt the water was turned to blood, even the water in jars and buckets. Can you imagine?"

Caleb shivered.

"Surely then Pharaoh knew that this was the work of God?" cried Asher.

"He said his own magicians could do the same, and would not listen, even though all the fish died and no one could drink water anywhere."

"Did this happen in Goshen, too, among our own people?" asked Asher, thinking of his wife and daughters.

When the man said, "No. Only among the Egyptians," Asher smiled and confidently proclaimed, "Then God is protecting us. Surely He will set us free."

The old shepherd went on, "And then…the frogs came."

"Frogs!" exclaimed Caleb.

"They were everywhere — climbing out of the great river, hopping in all the streets, getting into clothes and food. They even say that the frogs were in the very palace of Pharaoh, and in his bed."

Caleb laughed out loud. He thought this was very funny. Frogs in Pharaoh's bed!

"But," said the younger shepherd, with impatient sarcasm, "Pharaoh's magic men said they could also make frogs appear in the land of Egypt, and they did."

"How could Pharaoh know where the frogs came from, whether from God or the magicians?" asked Asher scornfully, not liking the shepherd's tone. "This Pharaoh is as blind as he is hard. Can his magic men deceive him so easily?"

"If it gives him an excuse for not listening to God," came the reply, which Caleb interrupted.

"What happened to all the frogs? Are they still there?"

"No. Pharaoh promised he would allow our people to leave the land if Moses asked God to take the frogs away."

"Then we're free!" cried Caleb, his face lighting up with delight. They could go home. His mother could see his lamb. They would never have to live in fear any more.

The shepherds shook their heads. The old one said, "Moses prayed and the frogs began to die. People had to sweep them up in great piles—in the streets, in the fields, in the courtyards of the palace. The stink of dead frogs was so great that people could hardly breathe. But when the frogs were dead, Pharaoh lost his fear of God and changed the order."

"And the people are being made to work until their backs break and they fall down and die," added the young man bitterly.

"Will Pharaoh never let us go?" despaired Caleb.

"He will let us go," said Asher. "No one can defy God for ever."

"So you say," said the young man, "but I'm glad I'm a free man in these mountains and not one of the brick-makers in Egypt."

"You speak as though you have no more fear of God than Pharaoh has," Asher accused him.

"I go by what I see with my eyes and hear with my ears. For centuries our people have been slaves and God has ignored us. Now this shepherd Moses comes—one who was brought up as an Egyptian himself—and with his talk has made things much worse for our people."

He went on angrily, "If God really cared, if God really planned to help us, He'd strike Pharaoh dead for his false promises and his lies. But Pharaoh grows fat while our people die in misery. That's what I see and hear, brother, and until I see and hear differently I'll take care of myself, in these hills."

"God can hear you," Asher reminded him.

"God is deaf," the shepherd replied.

Caleb had never heard a man speak like this before and he was frightened. He saw that his father was shocked. He saw that the other shepherds didn't know whether to agree with their companion or not.

Caleb had always thought that his father was right about everything, but for the first time the terrible idea struck him, "Suppose my father is wrong?" If God was powerless, if his father was wrong, then nothing was what it had always been. Everything was a lie.

At that moment it was as though the bottom was falling out of Caleb's world. Heart and head pounded. He felt sick and he got up to run away, not wanting to hear any more.

Where was Isaac? Isaac was real. The things you could see and touch were more real than anything else, just as the shepherd said, and just then Caleb desperately needed the most real thing he knew, to hold on to.

Isaac was asleep, with his head over another sheep's back, but he woke up when Caleb called him, stretched and came to him. His white woolly back was a good place for Caleb to bury his tears.

That night, while the other men slept, Caleb and his father watched over all the sheep. Asher knew his son was troubled. For a long time he waited for him to speak but Caleb was stubbornly silent, too afraid to reveal what was in his heart.

But Asher knew and, in the end, he said, "You must trust God."

"But suppose God is deaf?" burst out Caleb. "What will happen to us? Can we never go home?"

"Pharaoh is deaf," Asher told him, "not God."

"But how do we know Moses is telling the truth? Perhaps that story about the fire in the bush was only a dream. He thought it was real when it wasn't."

"What's real?" asked Asher.

"The things you can see, the things you can touch. Like Isaac," Caleb added, almost defiantly.

"And when you see a lake where you know there is no lake, with trees round it, and tents and flocks? Is that real?"

He was reminding Caleb that you could see many strange things in the desert, in the blinding sun— things that weren't real, even though they looked it; and real things that looked unreal as the sun's rays twisted and melted them, or seemed to.

"Only a fool believes only what he sees with his eyes," said Asher. "Can you see love? Can you touch it? Can you say what color it is?"

Caleb shook his head and Asher went on, "It's best to trust God. We'll soon know if Moses has told us the truth or whether he only dreamed what he saw."

"But why does God let our people die?" Caleb wanted to believe his father. He wanted to trust God, but still he couldn't forget what that shepherd had said.

"When Curly was lost, did you go to look for her?" Asher asked him.

Caleb nodded, wondering what this had to do with God and Moses.

"Did you find her?"

"Yes, but she was dead—and half eaten."

"If she'd called out, would you have found her more quickly?"

Caleb remembered how long he had taken to find her, but she had strayed so far, and he had slept the night through instead of searching.

"I don't understand," he said.

"If she hadn't strayed so far, you would have saved her. You saved the lamb and brought him home. And God is coming to save us. We don't know why He takes so long. He doesn't reckon time in days and weeks as we do. Perhaps we've strayed too far. Perhaps we don't cry out loud enough. Perhaps only now our prayers have reached Him because, until we were desperate, we didn't begin to pray. Perhaps He is coming faster than we know."

As if aware of Caleb's guilt over Curly, of having spent the night in sleep instead of searching, he went on, "God doesn't sleep, my son. God works while we are in darkness. When God sets us free, that faithless shepherd will be left behind here in the hills. He'll still be a slave in Egypt when we are free men."

"Are we going to stay in the hills?" Caleb asked, the darkness melting from his heart as his father's words drove out his fear.

"We are going to go home," said Asher. "It's time to go home and wait for our God to do as He has promised."

Caleb grinned at him with excitement. These were the words he wanted to hear and he roused up Isaac and shouted at him, "Do you hear that, Isaac? We are going home."

"Baa," said Isaac in reply.

~8~

Caleb had forgotten so much about home. He had been snatched so suddenly away, at an age when all his surroundings were just taken for granted, that his only memories were already much faded.

He was very shy at being folded into his mother's arms again and almost felt himself too grown up to be thus overwhelmed by her love; and he stared back at his sisters, whose big brown eyes took in every detail of their older brother with great curiosity and a shyness that equaled his own.

For so long his only roof at night had been the stars that he felt very restless inside his mother's little house. Surely it had been much bigger than this before! He had a strong memory of the steps from the lower part, where the donkey slept, to the upper part where they ate and slept being much steeper, but his mother laughed and promised him that they had not changed.

"It's you that's changed, Caleb. You've grown tall and strong and handsome. What a fine son I have! The Lord has blessed us indeed."

These things greatly embarrassed Caleb. He didn't know how to reply. Deep down, his heart was bursting with joy, but he was too used to being alone, or among men, to know how to talk to his mother and sisters now. It was easier to talk to Isaac.

To his great joy his father allowed him to bring Isaac home. The rest of the sheep were kept in the village fold at night, but Isaac was too special for Caleb to abandon like this. He knew his lamb would be safe in the fold, but Isaac had never slept far from Caleb's side.

"He can sleep with the donkey," Asher had promised, so the Isaac lamb came home and was soon as much a part of the family as everyone else.

Caleb's sisters made a tremendous fuss of Isaac, which he thoroughly enjoyed. They brought him bits of reed to nibble, and sweet things which he loved. They petted him and tried to ride on his back, and ran about squealing with laughter at all that he did and every sound that he made.

Caleb tried not to be jealous. He thought Isaac only cared about him. But Isaac liked everyone, and he particularly liked all the fuss Caleb's sisters gave him.

The first night at home Isaac just wouldn't stay with the donkey. He kept jumping up the steps and no one could get any sleep until Asher at last said to Caleb, "You'd better sleep with the donkey, too."

Caleb found a corner not too close to the donkey, in case he kicked, and he tried to persuade Isaac to lie down beside him. But Isaac was restless, perhaps because he could sense Caleb's own restlessness, too.

Caleb could hardly believe that he was home again —that he had sat at the low table with all his family, and dipped into the same dish with them, his mother's eyes upon him, hardly able to leave his face, except to gaze at her husband from time to time.

When everyone else had lain down to sleep on their mats, and Caleb had settled with the lamb and the donkey, he watched his mother carefully trim the oil lamp before lying down, too. The lamp was set on a small stand made from a tree branch and, as Caleb watched, the memory came flooding back to him of how his mother used to trim the wick every night, to make sure the lamp never went out.

How dark it would be if there were no light in the little house. It was only a very small light, feeding on the oil in which the wick floated, and Caleb was fascinated by the shadows that were cast by its steady flame—such big shadows, such gentle light, such comfort.

Sometimes, in the desert, when the moon was hidden behind clouds, the night was very dark. Caleb was frightened of the dark. It made him think of death, and death frightened him because he could not understand it.

His father said that God breathed life into all living things. That was how He had made the world— shaping things out of dust and breathing life into them. When they died they became dust again because God's breath was no longer in them.

Caleb had seen many a dead animal and, above all, he remembered their staring eyes, which somehow looked more dead than any other part of them.

When he saw the brightness in Isaac's eyes, he understood that everything that was in Isaac's nature —his curiosity, his liveliness, his determination, his teasing, playing, begging—all these things were mirrored in his eyes.

Dead eyes were like stones, hard, cold. If you looked into them you got nothing back but shock, or hurt, or a feeling of emptiness. Where did the life go when it was gone?

His father said God took it back. He gave everything, and He took it back.

Caleb had said, "It must be very dark when you're dead."

But Asher replied, "Not if you have God's light within you. His light never goes out."

Caleb couldn't remember a time when his mother's lamp had ever gone out. By its small light he could see his family fast asleep, the few bits of furniture removed to a corner to make space for their mats on the floor. He could see the donkey, who hardly slept at all except to doze with hanging head and flopping ears, now and again changing his weight from one leg to another. And he could see Isaac, who had settled at last and was lost in cud chewing.

It comforted him to know that even when you were dead it wouldn't be dark. If his mother always kept that lamp alight then surely God, who was so much more powerful, would keep His light burning, too.

Caleb's father didn't need to take the sheep very far to pasture them. There was good grazing land round the village and, because of all that had happened, the Egyptian people left them alone.

Caleb and his father soon learned that there had been other plagues since the last news they had received from the shepherds in the hills.

After the frogs had come a plague of gnats which had pestered both humans and cattle unmercifully— but only among the Egyptians and not among their own people. This time Pharaoh's magic men had said, "This is the finger of God," because they had tried to do the same magic but couldn't. Then they understood that Moses didn't do magic either. He just prayed, and God sent the gnats.

But still Pharaoh's heart was hard, so a plague of flies had come which drove the people to despair. There were flies everywhere, on the ground, in the houses, even in Pharaoh's palace and all over the people's faces.

This time Pharaoh said he would let the people go and even now Moses was talking to him and his officials, planning to take everyone on a three day journey into the desert to worship God and make sacrifices to Him.

There was great hope among the older men and great excitement everywhere. People waited from day to day for the command to come. The Egyptians made no efforts to molest them. In fact, they kept out of their way. They could see that their own gods had no power over this Hebrew God, whose name could never be mentioned, and they were frightened. Some were even trying to make friends with the slaves, asking questions about God, wanting to please Him.

It was a bewildering time, but an exciting one, and even Caleb's father, usually so calm and unruffled, was affected by it all. He spent hours talking to the other men. They prayed and sang praises to God, and waited for news from Moses.

Underlying every daily happening—going for water, making bread, feeding the donkey, pasturing the sheep, playing with Isaac, eating together at night, seeing the lamp lit, lying down to sleep—echoed God's command to Pharaoh, "Let My people go."

Caleb felt warm inside when he understood that

when God said "My people" it included him. There was something special about belonging to God. It stopped him feeling afraid, at a time when there was a great deal of fear and restlessness everywhere.

Again Pharaoh changed his mind, and God sent a plague upon the livestock throughout all Egypt. Everywhere cattle and sheep and goats, horses, camels and donkeys began to die.

Caleb saw whole flocks of sheep belonging to Egyptian shepherds lying stiff and dead in the fields. The black she-donkey belonging to an Egyptian widow who lived just down the street had foaled three days before. She fell sick and died, all in one day, and the foal died, too.

Caleb saw them both and shuddered with sorrow and fear. He remembered how the foal had been prancing with flicking tail, all head and legs, only the day before.

He was afraid for Isaac. Suppose the illness was catching? How could he bear to see Isaac sicken and die so suddenly? How could God know which sheep belonged to the Egyptians and which to the people of Israel? Suppose Isaac strayed into an Egyptian house? Would he die?

His father saw his fear and said, "Do you think our God doesn't know and care for that Isaac lamb as well as He knows and cares for you?"

Caleb was ashamed of his fear and lack of trust. "But why does He kill the animals?" he asked. "Is it their fault?"

"No. Pharaoh is to blame. None of this would happen if Pharaoh would just do as God commands."

"Why doesn't he then?"

"He's too proud."

Asher could see that Caleb didn't understand. Suddenly he asked, "Do you remember when Curly disappeared?"

Caleb nodded, wondering what this had to do with Pharaoh's pride.

"What stopped you from coming to tell me about it, just as soon as she was lost?"

Caleb stared at his father. A hot blush tinged his cheeks as a mixture of resentment and shame rose up within him, making his heart burn afresh. Why did he bring that up again? Would he never forgive him? Would he never forget?

His father's knowing eyes seemed to see right into his heart as he said, quite gently and without reproach, "Those same feelings are in Pharaoh's heart. He knows he's done wrong. He can't bring himself to admit it. He makes a thousand excuses—'It's not my fault. It's God's fault for making things so awkward for me.'"

"How can it be the same?" asked Caleb. "Curly was only a sheep."

"The things in your heart that stopped you coming to me to admit you'd done wrong are the same things that stop Pharaoh from coming to God. You came in the end to tell me Curly was lost because you had no choice. Would you have told me if there was any way I'd have found out otherwise?"

Caleb looked at the dust on the ground. Filled with shame, he shook his head. How wise his father was. How much he knew. It hurt to admit you were wrong about something.

"The bigger the wrong, the harder it is to confess it," said Asher. "But until we give in and admit we're wrong, things can't be put right. If you'd come to me sooner, Curly might not have died."

"God is very hard," said Caleb.

"Was I so hard with you that you couldn't come and tell me about Curly? Did you fear me so much that you couldn't talk to me?"

"No," admitted Caleb at last, chewing his lips with anguish and shame as he began to understand that the wrong had all been on his side.

His father had told him to do something. He had disobeyed, not on purpose, but he had disobeyed. Curly had died because he hadn't done what his father had told him to do. Pride had made him angry with his father, and blinded him to everything else.

Even now pride was in him, making it hurt when he had to admit that he was to blame. Even now he wanted to say that it was his father's sternness that had kept him from telling.

"I was angry because you didn't tell me," Asher said, knowing his thoughts. "If you had told me at the beginning, I would have understood and forgiven you."

"And is God the same?" asked Caleb, wanting so much to understand.

Asher nodded. He put his hand on Caleb's head in a gesture of warmth.

"I forgave you about Curly just as soon as you told me, even though I was angry. But you had to learn, my son. I was awake all night, praying for you."

"Were you really?" exclaimed Caleb, a smile bursting through his crestfallen expression.

"And didn't I show you that you were forgiven by letting you keep the Isaac lamb for yourself? Would I have given him to you if I didn't trust you?"

"And is God like that?" asked Caleb again, his heart filled with love for his father as he understood.

"God is much greater than we are. So His love is much greater than ours."

"Does He love Pharaoh, too?"

"He would love him, if Pharaoh would come to Him. But I fear very much that Pharaoh's heart is so hard and so proud that even more terrible things will happen before he finally admits that our God is right and he is wrong."

~9~

Caleb's father was right. There was so much hardness in Pharaoh's heart that, in spite of the suffering of his own people, his pride would not let him give way to God's command.

Soon after the death of so many animals, God sent a plague of boils upon the people of Egypt. Even Pharaoh's magicians were covered with boils, but they would not accept that this was the work of God.

"There's so much disease among us because of what has already happened," they explained. "This is why the boils have come."

So Pharaoh sent Moses and Aaron away and would have nothing to do with them.

By now it was winter and Caleb was glad to be home at night, remembering only too well the cold dark hours he had spent out of doors in previous years. It was good to be able to sleep on a mat with his parents and sisters, their feet just a few inches from the still warm hearthstone in the center of the room.

At first his eyes had wept at the smoke from the fire, which escaped only slowly through the few holes over the door, but bit by bit he grew hardened to the nuisance of it. Out in the crisp daylight, as soon as the sun had risen, the cold air cleared the smoke and encrusted tears from his eyes.

With nothing to shield him from the blustering winds but a goatskin jacket and a blanket wrapped round his shoulders, Caleb longed again for the warm little house, even though he would cough and splutter and find it hard to breathe. He went home each night stiff with cold, but Isaac had a coat so thick that Caleb would bury his fingers in it to find the warmth that clung close to Isaac's skin, deep under the wool.

It was just as well that Isaac now had this thick coat of wool because he was no longer allowed to sleep in the house. He had become so troublesome, always running into the neighbors' houses and poking his nose into what didn't concern him, that he was very unpopular at times.

He had broken jugs and dishes; stolen bread and milk; eaten up the grass brought home for the fire; chewed holes in bed mats; had a fight with the donkey; and altogether made a nuisance of himself. He wasn't a small lamb any more. He was almost as big as the older rams and his horns were already as long as his ears, curling backwards and downwards in a very shapely way.

On the day he made the donkey lame, after ramming him with his hard head, Caleb's mother complained, "He's too big now to stay with us. He's not a baby any more."

Anxiously Caleb looked at his father.

"Your mother's right," Asher agreed. "That lamb is almost full grown and it's time he learned to live with the sheep, and not with us. It'll do him good to be put in his place by the older rams. He's getting too cocky for his own good. He needs to learn a few lessons."

Caleb knew that his father was right. Only a little while ago he wouldn't have been able to imagine being separated from his lamb, but now he could accept his father's words without too much regret. He no longer needed Isaac's company as he had before. He had his mother and his sisters, other boys now, and, above all, there was this constant expectation of being on the move soon, leaving this land of Goshen for good.

During the day time, Isaac always grazed near him, coming up to him for tidbits and a brief game. But Isaac himself was losing his playfulness and looking to his own kind for company, more than to the boy. It was as if both of them recognized that childhood was over.

Spring came and the people began to speak hopefully again. Surely this year Pharaoh would set God's people free. Where was Moses? Would he come again with another message from God?

Moses did come again, and this time he came with greater power than before and with terrible words from the Lord.

"By now I could have stretched out My hand and struck you and your people with a plague that would have wiped you off the earth," were God's words for Pharaoh, and even stronger words than these.

"Let My people go, or this time I will send the full force of My plagues against you, so that you may know there is no one like Me in all the earth."

But still Pharaoh mocked and just when the land was beginning to yield its first harvest—with the barley fat-headed and bowed in the fields, and the flax in bloom—God sent a plague of hail upon the land of Egypt such as never had been heard of in the memory of any man.

The hail beat down everything growing in the

fields. The trees were stripped of their leaves, the harvests were destroyed. Animals died in the open, killed by giant hailstones. Men out in the fields died, too.

Caleb only heard of these things, for in the land of Goshen, where his people lived, the sun still shone and the harvest was good.

"God's blessing is on you people," said the Egyptians who lived in Goshen to the people of Israel, and they themselves railed against Pharaoh for the hardness of his heart.

Still Pharaoh would not bend. "We have the wheat harvest to come," he reminded his officials. "Our people won't go hungry."

But then God sent an east wind blowing over the land of Egypt, all day and all night. And the wind brought yet another plague, the most dreaded of all. Locusts.

They seemed like mountains in the sky, people said. Never had there been so many of them in all the history of Egypt. Men couldn't walk in the fields, which were black with them. Everything the hail hadn't destroyed was eaten by the locusts, but in the land of Goshen not a single locust was seen.

Ruin lay over the land of Egypt, but even then Pharaoh would not let God's people go.

The elders in the village could hardly believe that Pharaoh could be so hard. The Egyptians came to them and begged them to go. They offered them silver and gold, if only they would leave the land.

"How can we go without permission? Pharaoh would have us put to death," they replied. "No. Pharaoh will bend to our God, and then we will go."

It was a strange and frightening time for everyone, Egyptian and Hebrew alike. But the Lord blessed His people, even as He cursed the Egyptians.

Lambing time was over and there was a good increase in the size of the flock. Caleb worked willingly and he was often left in charge of the sheep on his own. The men of the village spent a lot of time in discussion and prayer these days and Asher was among them.

How proud Caleb was the first time his father put him in charge. The sheep knew him well now. They knew his voice as well as his father's and began moving towards him just as soon as he called.

It was exciting to have the responsibility of deciding where to take them; to decide where the best grazing could be found; and to have the job of counting them all safely back into the fold at dusk, watching out for any that might be ill or lame.

Caleb could hardly believe that a whole year had passed since Isaac was born, since the day he had found the orphaned lamb bleating in the thorn bush. But here were the new season's lambs to prove it, skipping about with high-pitched bleats as once Isaac had done, lanky and bouncy as he had been, shivering with curiosity at every new thing, chasing each other and playing king of the castle.

Isaac himself was a yearling now, as handsome a youngster as any shepherd could hope to have in his flock. His wool was thick and ready for the first shearing. He still walked close to Caleb when they were on the move, keeping off any who would try to take his place. And even now the two of them would enjoy a short wrestling match, which usually ended up with Caleb in the dust.

Isaac was a powerful young ram, full of strength, and Caleb was full of pride and love when he looked at him. He had forgotten that there had ever been a time when he had hated the sheep and cried out, "I don't want to be a shepherd."

Now he was proud that his father trusted him enough to leave him in charge of the flock. He carried his own staff for pulling sheep out of trouble, or smacking them across the rump if they misbehaved. As he strode along, occasionally looking back to make sure that the sheep were keeping up with him, he saw himself as his father, firm and strong and able, with every animal in the flock looking to him for guidance.

It was a good feeling and he couldn't help breaking into a grin again and again. One day he would be leading his own flock, not his father's, but already he was a true shepherd.

Spring brought riotous color to everything, and the sheep greedily snaffled up wild flowers and lush grass that sprang up over the harvested barley fields. It was good to watch them graze so contentedly, not having to travel far from home. It was good to watch the lambs playing themselves into weariness, then falling down in a bunch to sleep.

A call to Isaac. He would lift his head, still munching, and gaze at him. Yes, Isaac didn't forget him, even now.

One day Caleb went home to hear everyone talking about the great darkness that had come over the land of Egypt, sent by God against Pharaoh.

"Such a darkness it was, they say that you could feel it, that you could touch it."

People shivered with horror and looked up at the sky, over which the darkness of dusk was beginning to creep. "Will it come upon us?" was the thought in every heart.

Even Caleb shivered. He was frightened of the dark. A darkness you could feel and touch! He remembered nights in the hills, when clouds had hidden the moon and every star. That was a darkness you could feel, a darkness you could touch. There was evil in darkness. Everyone knew that.

"What can it mean?" people asked each other.

The darkness had lasted for three days, until Pharaoh had once again called for Moses and agreed to let all the people leave the land.

"But not the flocks or the herds. They must stay here," he had said.

When Caleb heard this he ran the rest of the way home, terrified that his father would leave this land and not take the sheep with him.

"We'd be able to take some, wouldn't we?" he begged. "We'd be able to take at least one, wouldn't we?"

Asher laughed. "You mean, we'd be able to take Isaac, wouldn't we?"

Shamefacedly, Caleb nodded. Was it so wrong to think of Isaac first? How could he help loving him so?

"Moses replied that we cannot go without our flocks and our herds, and this time Pharaoh has forbidden Moses to return."

The three days of darkness over the land of Egypt had brought the greatest fear of all to the suffering people. What did it mean? What would happen next?

Everyone waited. Would Moses return? Pharaoh had promised to have him put to death if he came back and the messengers said that Moses had replied to Pharaoh, "Very well, I will never appear before you again."

"What does Pharaoh want?" the elders asked each other. "What is he waiting for?"

"He wants Moses to pay a great price for our freedom," one of them replied. "If we all leave, with our flocks and our herds, who will do the work? Who will build the palaces? Who will make the bricks?"

"You are right," they agreed. "Pharaoh will only let us go for a ransom."

"But what ransom can Moses give? He's only a shepherd."

"Our God will ransom us," another said. "A price will indeed be paid, but surely it will cost Pharaoh very dear."

~10~

The Lord said to Moses, "Tell the whole community of Israel...."

Hardly had the news of the great darkness reached the people where Caleb lived, when messengers came again, special messengers this time. They didn't bring rumors and hearsay and personal opinions, but a message for every Israelite from the Lord their God.

All the men were called to a meeting and Caleb stayed with the sheep, hardly able to breathe as he wondered what was happening at that meeting. His excitement bordered on fear. When the Lord spoke everyone was afraid.

Even the Egyptians were afraid. No one told them what was happening but they all knew. Above all they knew that Pharaoh had completely turned his back on God—that God who time and again had showed Himself to be more powerful than any god of their own. Surely he could not do such a thing and live?

The meeting went on into the night. It was a strange night, a night when few people slept, and yet a silent night because people were too excited or too afraid to speak. Even the dogs didn't bark that night, as if they too knew the weight of the words the messengers had brought from Moses to the people.

Asher came home at last and there was a special light in his eyes when, with carefully chosen words, he shared with his family the message that had come from

God Himself. His wife had to encourage him to speak, and Caleb was to remember that night for the rest of his life, more than he ever remembered the nights and days that followed—nights when he could not sleep, days when his heart was filled with despair.

Dreadful though those days and nights were—and more dreadful still that last night they ever spent in Goshen—it was this night that stayed with him to the end of his life, the night that his father came home looking like a different man, a stranger almost, as if somehow he had been touched by the presence of God.

At last Asher spoke, looking first at his wife, then at Caleb, and then at the two girls who were almost asleep, leaning against their mother. The faces of all were dark and shadowy in the dim glow of the oil lamp in their midst.

"Tonight each one of us begins a new life. This is the beginning of a new year, and this is the first month, and the first day of that month. This is what the Lord says."

"Speak, my husband," Caleb's mother had to encourage him, gripping his hand.

Caleb couldn't understand why his father needed this encouragement. Surely this was good news? Surely they had waited for this day for many generations? But he felt his heart pounding within him because there was something in his father's look that frightened him.

"A terrible time is coming to Egypt," he went on at last. "A time far darker than those three days of darkness. They were surely a last warning to Pharaoh, who said he would kill Moses if he came again.

"Well, now the curse is upon his own head, for God has said that He will pass through the land of Egypt fourteen nights from now. Every firstborn, both of men and animals, will die."

No one spoke. Such a thing could not be taken in and understood. Caleb's heart pounded even faster, as if it would burst right through his chest. God passing through the land! Bringing death! Could anything be more frightening than this?

"Our people will be saved," Asher went on slowly. "We will be saved by the blood of a lamb which must be painted on the doorposts of our house."

"Strange thing!" wondered Caleb's mother. "The blood of a lamb? How can that save us?"

"God has said He will see the blood on the doorframe, and when He sees it He will pass over our house and not let death enter in."

"And what about our neighbors?" whispered Caleb's mother, as if to speak of these things in a louder voice would be far too painful.

"Only those protected by the blood will be safe." Asher then went on to explain many other things that must be done concerning food and how it should be prepared and eaten that night. Caleb was so frightened, so tired and so bewildered that none of these things remained in his head, except that everything had to be eaten in haste. They must be ready to leave Egypt immediately, perhaps in the middle of that dark night— whenever the word was given.

His mother and father spoke late into the night, in low voices, but Caleb eventually laid his aching body on the mat, his heart choked within him, though he didn't know why.

There was such a sense of foreboding within him

that just then he wished that none of these things had ever happened. It was all haste and fear and whisperings. Just then, the life he had led on the plains and in the hills—free from every care but that concerning the sheep—seemed much preferable to the new life about to begin.

Everything he knew was coming to an end—now. There had been so much talk, so much expectation, that he couldn't really believe that the day at last had come, heralded in by death as God Himself passed through the land.

Death and darkness. The two things Caleb most feared, and God was in control of them.

Caleb couldn't remember if he slept that night or if all the words he heard and the pictures he saw were real or imagined.

He saw Abraham building an altar of stones in the wilderness while his son Isaac watched with puzzlement, asking, "But where is the lamb, father? We have everything for the sacrifice but the lamb."

And he heard Abraham reply, in his own father's voice, "God will provide the lamb, my son. Don't be afraid. Trust God."

It was his father, not Abraham, who piled up the stones for the altar and then made him lie down in the place of sacrifice.

"Only the blood of a lamb will save us," he heard his father—or was it Abraham, or himself?—say.

"Why? Why?" Caleb shouted out, sweating with fear. He didn't want to die.

Then he saw his mother's face, comforting him, so

perhaps he had fallen asleep and it was only dreams that had terrified him.

God commanded Moses to tell the people, "On the tenth day of this month each man is to take a lamb for his family, one for each household. The animals you choose must be year-old males without defect."

So the men of the village rushed to Caleb's father and anyone else who kept sheep or goats, wanting a lamb or a kid. Suppose there weren't enough for everybody? What then? Outside the sheepfold there was much arguing as tempers rose. Men pointed to animals they liked the look of, only to find they were females, or too old, or with some defect. Whatever they were given, they quarreled with the shepherds, each one wanting the very best.

Caleb stood at the gate of the fold, letting out each yearling as it was called for. Each was grabbed by eager hands and dragged away, struggling in terror, too frightened even to cry out. They couldn't understand what was happening and yet each one knew it was something bad.

"Why must it be like this?" Caleb asked his father. "How can the blood of a lamb save us from death?"

Asher could give him no good answer. "The ways of God are beyond our understanding, my son. Perhaps one day we'll know what it means. It must mean something very special because we have been told to remember and celebrate this coming time every year, forever."

"Forever?"

Caleb couldn't imagine what forever was like. God was the only "forever" he knew. Could you celebrate and remember one special day for as long as that?

The Isaac lamb was so white and beautiful that every single man cried out, "I'll have that one," just as soon as they set their eyes on him. Even though Asher shook his head again and again, they argued, pleaded, and grew angry with him, while Caleb's heart burned with indignation.

"You want that one for yourself, don't you?" they jeered at Asher. "The best for you, just in case."

Asher made no reply to their remarks, but their words fell on Caleb's heart like a stone.

"That's my lamb," he cried out at last, hating them all for their grasping hands.

To them the sheep were no more than beasts to be sacrificed. They didn't know their names or their characters. They hadn't slept with them, eaten with them, walked with them through barren lands and dark valleys. All they wanted was their blood, to save themselves.

Soon it was the tenth day of the month, when each animal had to be set aside in preparation for the sacrifice. There were only two suitable lambs left in the flock for Asher to choose from for themselves. One of them was Isaac.

This was why Caleb hadn't slept; this was why each passing day was more unbearable than the one that had gone before, even though each day brought them nearer to the freedom they had groaned for, generation after generation for four hundred years.

In four nights' time death would strike everywhere in Egypt, from Pharaoh's family to the humblest slave's, and as Caleb stared at his lamb—who stared back at him from the fold, looking so handsome with his curling horns and high-held head—he felt his heart crumpling up inside him.

~ 11 ~

Dusk was falling and it was time to go home. One of the lambs would have to go with them, to be specially cared for until the fourteenth day. Caleb was paralyzed with fear and dread. He waited for his father to choose.

But his father looked at him and said, "It would be wrong for me to choose between them. One lamb is yours and one is mine. You're a good shepherd now, Caleb. The choice is yours. Which of these two lambs is the best one we can offer to God?"

Only a short while ago Caleb would have proudly boasted that Isaac was the most beautiful lamb in all the world. How vain that boast sounded in his ears now. Was it really true? And if it was....

Didn't God know his heart? Could he really choose anything less than the very best for God?

Why couldn't his father choose? Why must it be him?

Even as he wretchedly sought for some way out of his anguish he knew there was no way, and that his father couldn't choose because he loved him. If he chose his own lamb it wouldn't be honest. If he chose Caleb's, then wouldn't Caleb hold it against him with bitterness in his heart?

Caleb looked at the ground so that his father wouldn't see the tears in his eyes. He called to Isaac and the lamb eagerly pushed his way through the rest of the flock, happy to be called. He trotted fearlessly down the street behind father and son, unlike those other sheep who had never learned to trust as he did. When he came through the door Caleb's mother looked up in surprise, but then she understood and said not a word.

The two girls crooned with delight at seeing Isaac again. For the next four days they played with him and fed him with tidbits, while their mother began to pack up their few possessions in readiness for the journey.

It was more than Caleb could bear.

He stayed away from home from dawn till dusk, caring for the sheep that were left, and whenever Isaac came up to him in the house he brushed him aside. How could you look with love and joy on a lamb that was going to die for you so soon and be eaten? Because that was the Lord's command, too. Not only to kill the lamb but to eat him, roasted whole over the fire inside their house.

Asher said nothing. He combed the tangles out of Isaac's wool himself and the lamb stood still and let him, though never had such a thing happened to him before.

"Doesn't he look beautiful?" Caleb's sisters cried. Indeed, he did look beautiful. Asher polished his horns with oil and even trimmed and oiled his hooves, and nobody scolded Isaac for anything that he did, even though he was soon poking his nose into everything once more.

The day of sacrifice came. Out in the fields, father and son didn't speak to each other at all. Caleb felt so hard and dry inside that even breathing was painful. He kept thinking that perhaps at the last minute God would provide a better lamb than Isaac, or a different way to save them.

But Caleb knew that Isaac was a perfect lamb and it was not for him to question God's way of doing things, mysterious though it might be and so very painful.

"Trust in God," his father had said, and he had to trust Him though he didn't understand. Otherwise, he wouldn't have been able to bear these days.

They took the sheep back to the fold early that afternoon. Asher checked each one very carefully, for the next morning they would begin the journey to the promised land. How far distant and where that land was, they didn't know, but the shepherd did know that a sheep with sore feet wouldn't be able to travel well.

The lambs had to be killed at twilight and Asher went home before the sun began to sink, to prepare for that task. Caleb wouldn't go with him. He hung about; pretending he had found a ewe with a stone in her hoof, and his father went home without him.

Caleb went to the edge of the empty barley field and sat down. He stared at a distant tree which grew darker against the sky as the sun went down. Its stark blackness, gradually melting into the creeping dusk, somehow brought all the pain and bitterness in Caleb's heart to the surface. He groaned out harsh sobs while tears ran unchecked down his face.

Then it seemed as though a voice in his heart said to him, "Wouldn't you give your life for the sheep? Hasn't the lamb given his life for you?"

Where did those words come from? Had his father said them to him? No. He remembered very clearly every word his father had spoken these last few days, and they were not his words.

The tree was hardly more than a shadow in the blue-blurred mist of the sunset now and somehow Caleb's pain had melted away, too, in those solitary moments on the edge of the barley field. He stood up, wondering at the words now so clear within him.

A life for a life.

That was God's law, his father had told him, and now he saw that God had indeed provided the lamb to save his life, even as once He had provided a lamb to save the life of Isaac, son of Abraham.

He ran home, longing to tell his father that now he understood. The houses of the village were shut up. Not a door was open anywhere and there was no one in the streets.

Suddenly Caleb remembered that in the darkness of the night the Lord would come. How dark it was already! The sun had gone.

At his own house his father was in the street, waiting for him. He held a little lantern which gave out a very dim light. But at least it was a light, glowing in the darkness, showing Caleb that he was there.

"Hurry up, my son. The food will soon be ready and we must eat in haste, as God commands us."

"Is the blood on the door?" Caleb asked.

Fear was growing now as he thought of what lay ahead in the black night.

His father lifted the lantern, but it was too dark to see. Suppose God couldn't see in the darkness, either? He might not know the blood was there. Then he and his father would die. They were both firstborn sons.

Asher must have known his anxiety. He put the lantern at his feet, then stood with his back to the door. Then he stretched out his hands so that they touched the door-frames on either side.

"Do you see where my head and my hands are?" he said to Caleb. "That's where the blood is, where our God commanded us to put it. It's like this on every house. Now, come inside and get ready. Everything must be done according to God's will."

Every day Caleb had told himself that he would not eat the meat of his lamb, that he would spit it out and refuse. But he saw the fear on his mother's face turn to joy as he came through the door. She had been so frightened for him, thinking he wouldn't come home, but Asher had refused to go and look for him.

"He must come of his own accord," he had told her. "He must eat freely. The lamb is dead, but we can't force him to share in the sacrifice."

When Caleb saw that look; when she pulled him into her arms and hugged him so tightly so that he knew how much she loved him and how afraid she had been, he knew he couldn't refuse.

Perhaps Isaac hadn't understood why people he trusted had suddenly turned against him; why his own had killed him; why Caleb had abandoned him: but Caleb knew. It was for his sake and for the sake of his people.

This was meant to be a bitter time, even though the rejoicing would come later. A ransom was being paid —life for life—and many people would die because they had not listened to God. If he refused to eat, it would be as if he didn't accept the ransom. If he really loved his lamb, then he would eat the meat his mother had prepared, even though it was made salty with his tears.

So Caleb joined the circle with them, when each one was dressed for the journey. Everything they possessed was in bundles, ready to be fastened across the donkey's back. The donkey seemed to know this was a special night. He watched them all with pricked ears.

Caleb's mother had prepared bitter herbs and bread without yeast, according to God's command. These things were to remind them of the afflictions of their people from which they were being ransomed by the blood of the lamb that had died. Solemnly Asher explained all this. No one else said a word.

It was no night for talk. Outside there was a silence, too. No dogs barked, no sheep bleated, no donkey brayed. It was as if time was standing still and everything with it.

Suddenly, some time after midnight, there was a sharp cry of anguish, followed by another, and another. And then a wailing broke out from every side in the village—wives mourning for dead husbands, mothers weeping for dead sons, sisters sobbing for dead brothers, broken-hearted fathers crying out against Pharaoh for his wickedness in allowing this terrible calamity to come upon them.

All over Egypt that night there was weeping and wailing such as there had never been, from the palace of Pharaoh himself to the dungeons where prisoners died in their chains. In the middle of the night the Lord struck down all the firstborn, as He had promised.

"None of this would have happened," whispered

Caleb's mother—who wept herself for the sorrow in other women's hearts—"if they had listened to God."

Before dawn the bundles were packed on to the donkey's back. The two girls helped with this work while Asher and Caleb went out to prepare the sheep. There was no time to lose. Just now the Egyptians were too grief-stricken to care what was happening around them—except to shower them with gifts and plead with them to go. But who knew if Pharaoh might not stop them once more?

The sheep were surprised to see the shepherds so early. Dawn was only a vague hint among the stars, not yet strong enough to dispel the darkness, and they were still lying down in small groups. It was a much smaller flock now. The best yearling males were gone. Only those with defects and the older males remained and, of course, the females, most of which had a lamb at foot.

Caleb had gone out with his father into the deserted street filled with an excitement that was almost a pain. The sharp air, not yet softened by the sun to come, was as keen as his anticipation.

There was a new kind of joy in his heart. This was a very special day, the first day of freedom. His people were slaves no more. They could lift up their heads and shout aloud and not be afraid. They were going to start a new life in a new land. Nobody yet knew where that land was. All they knew was that God would lead them and that Moses was indeed God's voice among them.

It was only when he reached the fold that Caleb's joy was momentarily checked. Isaac's name rose automatically to his lips. Every morning he called to him.

Every morning he looked to see that white, woolly head, with its proudly curling horns, look up from among the rest. When he reached the gate Isaac was always already there, ears pricked, eyes alert, every bit of him eager to return the greeting.

The name died on Caleb's lips. His father looked at him. He knew what was in his son's heart.

He said, "We must sort out the lambs. You must choose two for yourself. After all, you're a shepherd now and you can't be a shepherd without sheep."

They stood at the gate and Asher let Caleb call out their own animals from among all those gathered there. He knew all their names now and, more important still, they recognized his voice and came when he called them. A year ago they would have ignored him.

Now they came hurriedly, mothers hustling their lambs, all bleating impatiently. There were a couple of white lambs among them, and Caleb was tempted to say, "I'll have them," because they would remind him of Isaac.

But he held his tongue, realizing that a good shepherd chooses with greater care. He would wait and watch as the days went by. He would see which were the strongest, which could bear up to the traveling best. If he chose weaklings, then he would never get a good flock together. It would be wrong to choose a lamb just because it looked like Isaac.

Isaac had been a very special lamb, given to him by God for a very special purpose. He knew there would never be another lamb like Isaac, who had died to give him life. He would remember him always, but he didn't need to be ransomed again.

92

Although there was sorrow, because of past things that couldn't be any more, in that night of darkness—when the Lord had passed over the land of Egypt ransoming His people—Caleb had grown up. The old life was over, a new life was beginning. Isaac was still with him in his heart and would be with him always.

Caleb smiled and returned his father's look. He was ready to face whatever lay ahead.

About the Author

Helen Santos began writing when she was five years old. She had her first book published when she was still a teenager in the 1950's. Since then she has had about thirty books published, primarily for children. Helen has a real love for animals, which also is portrayed in many of her books. The majority of her books were published under her maiden name, and have been translated into many languages, including Hebrew and Icelandic.

Helen married a Spaniard, had three daughters and lived in Spain for twenty years. After Helen lost her husband in a tragic car accident, she and her three daughters returned to England for a new start. It was after the conversion of her eldest daughter at the age of seventeen that Helen also came to know Christ. This was the time in her life that *Caleb's Lamb* was written.

Helen now has thirteen grandchildren and is very active in church life. One of her greatest enjoyments is running the weekly children's club for four to nine-year-olds. As Helen reflects on her life she says, "It's a great privilege to tell children about Jesus, and the best thing of all is when they stop me on the street to ask me things about God."